Quick Change

by Erin Falligant

illustrated by Arcana Studios

★ American Girl®

Published by American Girl Publishing
Copyright © 2012 American Girl

Questions or comments? Call 1-800-845-0005,
visit **americangirl.com**, or write to Customer Service,
American Girl, 8400 Fairway Place, Middleton, WI 53562-0497.

Printed in China
12 13 14 15 16 17 18 LEO 10 9 8 7 6 5 4 3 2 1

Illustrated by Thu Thai at Arcana Studios

Welcome to Innerstar University! At this imaginary, one-of-a-kind school, you can live with your friends in a dorm called Brightstar House and find lots of fun ways to let your true talents shine. Your friends at Innerstar U will help you find your way through some challenging situations, too.

When you reach a page in this book that asks you to make a decision, choose carefully. The decisions you make will lead to more than 20 different endings! (*Hint:* Use a pencil to check off your choices. That way, you'll never read the same story twice.)

Want to try another ending? Read the book again—and then again. Find out what would have happened if you'd made *different* choices. Then head to www.innerstarU.com for even more book endings, games, and fun with friends.

Innerstar Guides

Every girl needs a few good friends to help her find her way. These are the friends who are always there for **you.**

Emmy

A brave girl who loves swimming and boating

Isabel

A confident girl with a funky sense of style

Riley

A good sport, on the field and off

Paige

A nature lover who leads hikes and campus cleanups

Amber

An animal lover and
a loyal friend

Neely

A creative girl who loves
dance, music, and art

Logan

A super-smart girl
who is curious about
EVERYTHING

Shelby

A kind girl who is there
for her friends—and loves
making NEW friends!

Innerstar U Campus

1. Rising Star Stables
2. Star Student Center
3. Brightstar House
4. Starlight Library
5. Sparkle Studios
6. Blue Sky Nature Center

7. Real Spirit Center
8. Five-Points Plaza
9. Starfire Lake & Boathouse
10. U-Shine Hall
11. Good Sports Center
12. Shopping Square
13. The Market
14. Morningstar Meadow

[**S**] o, what do you think?" Logan asks, examining her reflection in the mirror at Bravo Boutique. She's dressed in a black velour cat costume with furry trim at the collar and cuffs. A long black tail stretches out behind her, swaying slightly as she turns from side to side.

"Wait!" says Neely. She smooths out Logan's brown bangs so that she can add the finishing touch: a headband with pointy pink and black ears.

"It's adorable," you say, "and it's so *you*, Logan." Your friend loves cats, maybe because they're curious about everything—just as she is.

Logan nods, satisfied, and does one more circle in front of the mirror. She's a smart shopper, always checking things out to make sure they really fit, but you can tell she's already sold on this costume. Her green eyes are dancing, and a smile plays at the corners of her mouth.

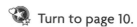 Turn to page 10.

Standing at the clothing rack beside you, your friend Shelby strokes the shimmering fabric of an angel costume.

"Oh, an angel! Try on the halo, Shelby," you nudge.

She blushes. "I shouldn't," she says. "I've already spent too much money today."

You know how that goes. You just blew two months' worth of allowance on a new scooter, and you still need to get a costume for Innerstar University's fall party. There must be *something* in here that you can afford.

You explore a rack of princess gowns and superhero capes, and then you see it—a genie costume made of deep purple satin. You're already envisioning yourself in the costume when you check the price tag: $39.95. *Gulp.* You don't have even half of the money you need.

"I'm going to make my own costume," Neely pipes up. "That way no one else in the world will have one like it."

"What are you going to be?" Shelby asks.

"I haven't decided," says Neely thoughtfully. "It'll be a surprise."

You examine the genie costume. Can you make one like it? Probably not, since the only thing you've ever sewn was a sock monkey. You can't afford the costume, but you can't bring yourself to put it back on the rack, either. What if someone else snatches it up?

 Turn to page 12.

"I'm going as a genie," you say firmly. "I just have to figure out how to make some money over the next few weeks."

"Bake sale!" Logan sings from the fitting room. She works at Sweet Treats bakery on campus, and she's always willing to bake a batch of treats for a good cause.

"You might make more money selling crafts at the Market," Neely suggests.

You're about to respond when you catch sight of your friend Megan parking her bike on the sidewalk outside the window. You remember Megan telling you that she just started a new job, delivering packages for stores in the Shopping Square. Suddenly, your mind is swirling with money-making ideas.

If you decide to hold a bake sale, turn to page 14.

If you make crafts to sell, turn to page 16.

If you look into making deliveries for stores, turn to page 15.

You decide to try the craft sale on your own. You're pretty sure you have all the skills and smarts you need to do it right.

After a quick run to Sparkle Studios to buy supplies, you sit down at your desk and start crafting. You decorate hair clips with sparkly rhinestones and colorful beads. You wrap headbands with soft, fuzzy yarn, and you spruce up scrunchies by tying on short strips of shimmering organdy ribbon.

After a few hours, your desk is already lined with rows of cute and creative hair accessories. You're pretty proud of your work, and you can't wait to see how it sells!

On Saturday, you set up a small table at the Market. All around you, girls are selling crafts, jewelry, and second-hand clothes on tables under brightly colored tents. The Market is teeming with shoppers, laughing and chatting. You can almost feel the buzz of energy in the air.

You make one last adjustment to the rainbow-colored spread of crafts on your table. Then you prop up the sign with your price list. Now you just have to wait for your first customer . . .

 Turn to page 23.

You've helped Logan raise good money selling cookies and other treats in the past, so a bake sale sounds like the perfect solution. That genie costume will be yours in *no* time.

"Where do you think I should have the sale?" you ask as Logan comes out of the fitting room, the cat costume draped over her arm.

She cocks her head, thinks for a moment, and says, "How about the Good Sports Center? There's a soccer game there tomorrow afternoon."

Perfect!

By the next afternoon—after emptying your piggy bank to buy baking ingredients and spending all morning baking with Logan—you're setting up your bake-sale table near the entrance to the sports center. While you arrange your chocolate chip cookies in tidy rows, you notice that there are three *other* girls selling snacks near the soccer field. Who knew you'd have so much competition?

 Turn to page 17.

You've done your share of bake and craft sales. Making deliveries for stores sounds much more exciting. Your bike chain is broken, so you can't use your bike, but you do have a brand-new, very expensive scooter you can use.

Now you just have to figure out how to start your delivery business. Maybe you could work with Megan, at least until you learn more about the business. Or would you make more money striking out on your own?

If you ask Megan if you can work with her, turn to page 18.

If you start your own delivery business, turn to page 21.

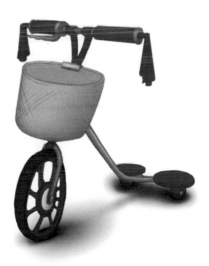

A craft sale sounds like fun to you. You just took a workshop at Sparkle Studios and learned how to make some cool hair accessories, and you think they're cute enough to sell.

You go back to your room that afternoon and make a list of the supplies and other things you'll need for your sale. At the end of your list, you write "partners?" You haven't decided yet whether you want to do this on your own or with a friend or two.

Would you make more money on your own or with friends? Would it be fun to work with friends, or would you disagree about how to do things? You're just not sure.

 If you try the sale first on your own, turn to page 13.

 If you invite some friends to be "business partners," turn to page 22.

As the soccer game starts, you feel a flutter of excitement, anticipating all the customers who might come to your table. But by halftime, you've sold only *three* cookies. The second half is kind of a wash, too.

After the game, you cross your fingers, hoping that some of the players will stop by. You recognize your friend Riley walking off the field in her bright blue jersey and blonde ponytail. She waves at you. She's heading your way!

But . . . *wait.* Now she's stopping at one of the other snack tables. By the time she reaches your table, she's already halfway through a bag of pretzels that she bought from someone else.

"How're things going?" Riley asks, wiping a few crumbs from her chin.

You hesitate before answering. The truth is, things aren't going well at all, and you're kind of hurt that Riley bought snacks from someone else instead of from you. Do you cover up your hurt and pretend all is well, or do you tell her the truth?

If you tell Riley the truth about how your sale is going, turn to page 20.

If you pretend that business is good, turn to page 26.

You catch Megan as she's leaving a store called Dream Décor and climbing back onto her bike.

"Hey, Megan!" you call to her.

She glances up, tossing her black hair over her shoulder, and waves.

"Sorry, I don't have time to talk," she says hurriedly. "I have to make a delivery."

"I know," you say. "That's what I want to talk to you about. Do you think any of the stores you work for would hire me, too? I could sure use the money."

Megan tilts her head and thinks for a moment. "There's probably enough work for the two of us," she says. "Let's talk about it later, okay?"

 Turn to page 30.

"Actually," you say to Riley, counting the coins and bills in your money box, "I've made only—um—two-fifty so far. I can't figure out what I'm doing wrong."

You glance at the bag of pretzels in Riley's hand and feel another twinge of hurt. Riley blushes a little, dropping the bag down by her side.

"Your cookies look really good," she says quickly. "But our coach is always drilling us to eat healthier snacks after a game, so I went for the pretzels."

"Oh!" you say, suddenly feeling better. "That makes sense. Maybe I need to sell some healthy things instead of cookies."

Riley takes another look at your cookies. "Or maybe you could sell both?" she asks. "I mean, I need a healthy snack now, but I *have* to have one of those chocolate chip cookies for later," she says. "How much?"

 Turn to page 24.

You figure you'll make more money if you work alone, and the sooner you start, the better. You take a deep breath of courage and step up to the checkout counter.

"Excuse me," you ask the tall blonde girl behind the counter. "Do you ever hire students to make deliveries for you? I'd like to apply for the job."

The girl nods. "Sometimes we do," she says. "But do you have any experience?"

Uh-oh. You don't have any delivery experience, but you're afraid that if you admit that, you won't get the job.

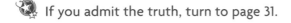

 If you make up a story about past experience, turn to page 25.

If you admit the truth, turn to page 31.

You decide to invite some friends to be your business partners, and who better than your shopping buddies—Neely, Logan, and Shelby?

You ask them over dinner at the student center, and they're all excited about your business venture.

"I have lots of craft supplies," says Neely.

"Me, too," Shelby pipes up.

"Great!" you say. "Why don't you all come to my room tonight and we'll get started?"

An hour later, your friends show up with supplies, as promised. But when the four of you pool your supplies in the middle of your bedroom floor, you realize that everyone brought the *same* thing: beads and glue, but no plain barrettes or other hair accessories. What will you do with all those beads if you don't have any barrettes to glue them on to?

You slap your forehead, realizing that as the leader of this business, you should have been more organized and told them what to bring.

"Sorry," you say to your friends. "I'll run out and buy barrettes. Let's try this again tomorrow."

 Turn to page 45.

Here comes a customer!

It's a girl you've seen around campus but don't know well. She has shoulder-length raven-black hair, and she chooses a bright red headband that you think will look great on her. "How much?" she asks.

"Five dollars," you say, pointing to your price list.

The girl's eyes widen. "That seems like a lot," she says. "There's someone else selling headbands for a dollar fifty over there." She points toward the other side of the Market.

"Oh," you say, not sure how to respond.

 If you drop your price to match the competition, turn to page 32.

 If you keep your price at five dollars, turn to page 34.

Over dinner that night at the Star Student Center, you talk with Logan and another friend, Paige, about Riley's idea. "So I'm going to come up with something healthy to sell, too," you say excitedly.

"That's cool that you got a tip from a 'customer,'" says Paige. "When it comes to business, it's smart to listen to other people's ideas." Then Paige launches into a business idea of her own: she's been leading nature hikes on the trails around Innerstar U. "Well, it's more of a volunteer thing," she says, "but it's still fun."

Trails? That gets you thinking about the perfect healthy snack: trail mix!

 Turn to page 27.

It's smart to listen to other people's ideas.

"Actually," you say to the girl, "I used to make deliveries all the time at home—before I came to Innerstar U."

The girl smiles. "Great!" she says. "We'll just need you to write down the names and phone numbers of the businesses you delivered for." She hands an application form and a clipboard over the counter.

Now you have to think fast. "Um, can I take the form with me?" you ask. "I don't have the phone numbers here."

"Sure," the girl says, sliding the application out from under the clasp of the clipboard. "Bring it back anytime."

You don't remember much about the walk back to your room. Your heart is pounding, and guilt gnaws at your conscience. You lied about having experience, and now you're stuck. You can't make up names and numbers, so you won't be able to bring the form back to Bravo Boutique. And you're pretty sure that if you apply at another store, you'll run into the same problem: you just don't have any experience!

Your shoulders droop. *I guess it's time for plan B,* you think. *B for bake sale.* You can't bring yourself to get excited about that idea right now, though. Maybe tomorrow.

The End

"The sale is going great," you tell Riley, closing the lid of the cash box so that she won't see how *not* great your profits are so far.

"Oh, good," she says. "Then we'll probably see you here again for tomorrow's game?"

Tomorrow? You didn't know there was another game scheduled, but given how many cookies you have left over, you're going to have to come back tomorrow just to try to get rid of them.

"Definitely," you say, with more confidence than you actually feel.

Turn to page 33.

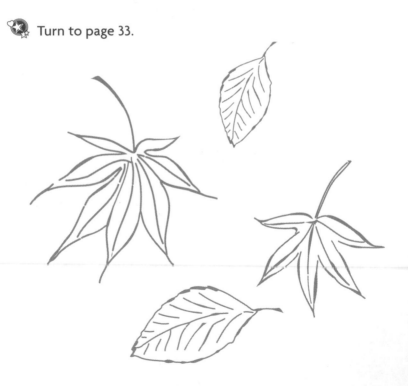

You can picture it now—you'll mix nuts, raisins, cereal, and chocolate chips in cute little pouches and decorate them with stickers that say "Happy (and healthy!) trails."

You talk with Paige a bit more about her nature hikes. "Can I set up my snack table near the Blue Sky Nature Center, where your hikes start?" you ask her.

"That's a great idea," she says. "And I'll make sure to lead hikers past your table. I'm leading a hike tomorrow morning. Can you be there?"

"Yes!" you say, already thinking about how many bags of trail mix you'll need to prep. You'd better get busy!

 Turn to page 28.

On Sunday, you set up shop outside the nature center. Your table is piled high with cookies and bags of trail mix.

Paige leads a group of hikers by your table, and other students stop by, too. You sell a *lot* of trail mix—and plenty of cookies. You make over seventeen dollars, which feels like a fortune after your last sale.

You're so excited that you decide to keep selling. There's another soccer game today, so midafternoon, you set up your table at the sports center. You advertise your healthy trail mix, and you add a new specialty: lemonade. A sign in front of the lemonade reads, "Delicious and nutritious!" The lemonade came from a powdery mix, but there must be lemons—and vitamin C—in there somewhere, right?

Shelby is at the game taking pictures, and she stops by for lemonade. "Nutritious?" she says. "That's great. Did you make this from real lemons—with less sugar?"

"Um, no," you admit, "but lemonade is lemonade, right?"

Shelby shrugs. "Most lemonade has lots of sugar in it, that's all," she says. "I wouldn't exactly call it nutritious."

Huh. Is Shelby accusing you of false advertising? You're not sure how to respond.

 If you take down your sign but keep selling lemonade, turn to page 36.

If you think of a healthier drink to sell, turn to page 50.

If you leave your sign up, turn to page 43.

"Thanks!" you say, turning on your heel and jogging back into Bravo Boutique. You give your genie costume one last adoring look. "You'll be mine before you know it," you whisper.

You catch up with Megan in her room at Brightstar House later that day. She says that Dream Décor is one of her best customers because girls order rugs, pillows, and bedspreads in colors and patterns that are available only online. When they get shipped to the store, Megan picks them up and delivers them to the girls.

You decide to visit the store right away. You hop on your scooter and head to Shopping Square.

Dream Décor is full of cool merchandise, but you ignore it all and head straight for the checkout counter. You feel a rush of nerves in your stomach as you walk. You've never tried to get a job like this before, but Megan said it would be a piece of cake.

"Excuse me," you say to the cashier, a girl with auburn hair pulled into a low side pony. "I'm here to apply for a delivery job."

The girl smiles. "I know," she says. "Your friend Megan just called. She's one of our best workers, and she says that you will be, too. We can get you started right away."

Thank you, Megan! you think. You're sure glad you talked with her first.

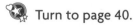 Turn to page 40.

"I don't have any experience," you admit. "But maybe you could give me a chance? I could do some deliveries for free, just to see how it goes."

The girl raises an eyebrow, and then she smiles. "I like that idea," she says. "I think we might be able to work something out." Then she reaches her hand across the counter and introduces herself. "My name is Natalie. Nice to meet you."

Natalie calls you with a job right away the next day. A student bought a costume at the boutique but needed to have the hem shortened. The costume is ready for delivery, so you hop on your scooter and rush to the boutique. Natalie greets you at the door with a small wrapped package.

The package fits into the basket of your scooter, and away you go toward room fifty-two at Brightstar House. You get a signature from the red-headed girl who opens the door, and then you head back to Bravo Boutique as fast as you can to give Natalie the signed form.

She's impressed with your speed, so she gives you another job. "This time," she says, "I'll pay you." Your heart leaps!

 Turn to page 35.

"Well, a dollar fifty is okay, I guess," you say with a shrug. "Actually, make that one dollar even." If your prices are lower than the competition's, you're bound to sell more, right?

"Really?" the girl says, smiling. "Great! I'll take two."

You change the price on your sign, and as the afternoon wears on, you sell a lot more headbands. When you finally run out of them, you celebrate. What a success!

That night, you take the money you earned and visit Sparkle Studios to buy more supplies. Then you stay up an hour past your bedtime decorating headbands in the hope that you can sell more at the Market tomorrow.

Turn to page 37.

The next afternoon, you get to the sports center early to scope out a better spot to set up your table. You aren't early enough, apparently, because two other tables are already there. *Sheesh,* you think to yourself. *Did they camp out overnight?*

You sell a few cookies to some swimmers leaving the sports center, but you spend most of the first half of the game alone at your table, wondering what you're doing wrong.

Shelby is taking photos of the game, and she stops by your table at halftime. "Say cheese!" she says, raising her camera.

You put on a happy face—for Shelby's sake, because she's always so positive. You think back to the costume she was looking at in Bravo Boutique and ask, "Hey, have you bought that angel costume yet?"

Shelby shakes her head. "I can't afford it," she says, "but it might be fun trying to make my own costume this year."

You nod. The way it looks, you might be doing the same. You spend the second half of the game imagining what your costume will be. A soccer player? A baker, with apron and cap? A hobo, with nothing to her name but a bag full of cookies? You'll figure something out. If Shelby can look on the bright side, so can you.

The End

You don't want to lose a customer, but you remember how hard you worked on decorating the headbands. They turned out really well, and you're proud of your work. You think the headbands are worth five dollars.

Your customer must agree, because she ends up buying the headband—and puts it in her hair right away to wear around the Market. You sell three more that afternoon, which makes you feel good about leaving the price as is. Your last customer is Shelby, who buys a white headband and some sparkly barrettes.

Shelby sticks around to help you take down your table for the day. Just as you're carefully sliding your remaining hair accessories into a box, the dark-haired girl who bought the red headband shows up at your table. She's holding the headband in her outstretched hand.

"I changed my mind about the headband," she says. "Can I get my money back?"

You're speechless. You saw the girl wearing the head-band all afternoon. Is it fair for her to return it to you now?

 Turn to page 42.

You do a few more jobs for Bravo Boutique, but they don't need too many deliveries, so your savings aren't growing quickly.

When you bump into Logan outside the library, she asks how business is going. "Honestly," you say, "I need more work, or I'll never have that costume in time for the party."

Logan gazes off toward the student center. "Sometimes my manager at Sweet Treats bakery needs cupcakes delivered," she says. "Her name is Jessica. You should go talk to her."

You take Logan's advice right away. You jog toward the bakery and ask the girl behind the counter if you can talk to the manager about doing deliveries. You're nervous, but not nearly as nervous as you were the first time you asked for work—at Bravo Boutique.

Jessica comes out of the back kitchen wiping her hands on a towel. The first thing she asks is, "Do you have any experience?" This time you're able to proudly say "YES."

Jessica does have work for you, and that afternoon, you make your first delivery: a dozen cupcakes to Real Beauty Salon for someone's birthday.

The cupcakes are hard to deliver on a scooter. You have to arrange them in three small boxes that you stack carefully in your basket. You scooter very, *very* slowly with your precious cargo.

 Turn to page 44.

"I guess you're right," you say to Shelby, suddenly feeling embarrassed. You sigh and reach across the table to take down the lemonade sign.

You can tell that Shelby feels bad now. A worried look flashes across her brown eyes, and she says quickly, "Your lemonade is delicious, though. Can I have another cup?"

"Sure," you say, lifting the pitcher. "But this one's on me." Shelby protests, but you hold up your hand to keep her from dropping another quarter in your money box. "It's a thank-you—for the good advice," you add with a smile.

After Shelby leaves, you have a steady stream of other customers. Your trail mix is a big hit. You sell a few cups of lemonade, too, but most of the soccer players have water bottles with them already. Ah, well . . . lesson learned, right?

 Turn to page 38.

On Sunday, you have another successful sale. The headbands are your best-selling product, so you're pretty sure you'll be making a lot more. But then it hits you: if you keep spending all of your money on supplies for headbands, when will you actually start *making* money?

You're chewing on that thought when your friend Isabel stops by your table. She's always dressing up her curly red hair with funky accessories, so you're not surprised when she reaches for a green headband and hands you five dollars.

"Thanks," you say, digging around in the money box for her change.

You must sound less than enthusiastic, because Isabel says, "What's wrong? You sound tired."

You explain your dilemma to her. "I'm just not sure when I'll start seeing a profit," you say.

Isabel scrunches up her forehead. "Well, let's see," she says. "How many headbands did you sell today? And how much did supplies cost for the headbands?"

You tell Isabel that you sold twelve headbands, and then you add up what you paid for supplies—nine dollars for the plain headbands, plus two-fifty for the yarn and another three dollars for the craft glue. Over fourteen dollars? You never added it up before, and suddenly it sounds like a lot.

Isabel listens, and then she laughs. "And you're selling each headband for a dollar?" she asks. "You'll never make money that way. You're actually *losing* money!"

 Turn to page 41.

After the game, Riley stands by your table for a while, munching on trail mix. "What a great postgame snack!" she says, swallowing a mouthful. "It's much better than pretzels," she adds with a grin. Then she reaches for her water bottle, but it's empty.

Riley turns the bottle upside down and shakes it. "Hmm," she says, eyeing the plastic pitcher on your table. "Can I have a cup of lemonade instead?"

You're thrilled. As you pour the lemonade, Riley fishes around in her pockets for money. She comes up empty-handed. "I think I left the rest of my money in my room," she says, her cheeks turning pink. "Can I pay you later?"

"No problem," you say. Riley is a good friend. Plus, you have lots of lemonade left. Why haul it all home with you?

"Ooh, cookies!" you hear someone say from over Riley's shoulder. It's dark-haired Becca, another soccer player. "I forgot my money, too," she says. "Can I pay you later?"

You hesitate. Now what?

 If you give Becca the cookie, turn to page 46.

 If you say no, turn to page 55.

Making deliveries on a scooter turns out to be hard work. You want to go fast so that you can deliver more packages, but if you take corners *too* fast, the packages might spill out of your basket. It takes a couple of days before you can cruise with confidence along the campus trails.

You go to Dream Décor three days in a row after classes to see if they have deliveries for you, and usually they do. By the fourth day, you're tired and your homework is piling up, but you go anyway.

As you park your scooter in front of the shop, you run into Megan, who doesn't look very happy to see you.

"I haven't made a delivery for Dream Décor all week," she snaps, "because you're doing all the work. I was hoping we could *share* the work."

Uh-oh. You don't want to upset Megan, but you want all the work you can get so that you can buy the genie costume before it sells out. Now what?

If you look for a way to share the work with Megan, turn to page 52.

If you tell her you need as much work as you can get, turn to page 56.

Isabel takes a minute to explain some basic business math: your income (what you charge) has to be more than your expenses (the cost of supplies), or you won't make a profit.

It sounds so simple, but now you're embarrassed. You wasted so much time—and money!

"Don't worry," says Isabel. "I can help you make it back. I'm pretty good at math and this business thing."

"Deal," you say, shaking her hand. You know now that you *do* need a business partner, and Isabel might be the one.

"First things first," she says, reaching for a marker. She flips over your price list and copies it onto the other side, changing the price of headbands from one dollar to three dollars. That sounds like a pretty fair price. This time, you'll be smart enough to *stick* with it.

The End

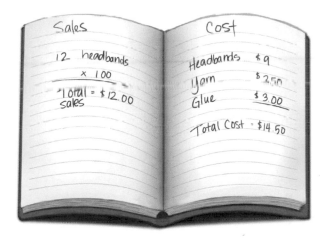

You're racking your brain trying to figure out how to handle the situation when Shelby suddenly speaks up.

"We're sorry you weren't happy with the headband," she says sweetly. "Is there something wrong with it?"

"Oh, no," says the girl. "I just remembered I need to save my money to buy a birthday gift for a friend."

Shelby talks fast. "We do have a no-refund policy," she says, "but you can exchange the headband for anything here. Maybe your friend would like a ribbon scrunchie or a beaded barrette?" Shelby reaches into the box and begins laying some of your other crafts on the table.

The girl examines the accessories and reaches for a rhinestone-studded barrette. "Actually," she says, "I bet my friend would love this one. She likes sparkly things."

"Great!" says Shelby. "Good choice. I really like that one, too."

 Turn to page 51.

You leave up your lemonade sign. It's just advertising, right? You've seen plenty of ads in magazines and store windows that exaggerate a little bit. *Maybe Shelby just doesn't understand business,* you think to yourself.

At halftime, some soccer players walk by your table. You decide to give this advertising thing all you've got. "Cookies! Trail mix! Lemonade—nutritious and delicious!" you call out as they pass.

One of the girls turns to look, and when she sees your cookies, she stops walking. "Wait a sec," she says to her teammates. "I think I need a snack." As she's choosing a cookie, the other soccer players mill around your table, including Becca, one of the best players on the team. She checks out your lemonade sign.

"Nutritious and delicious," she says in a singsong voice. "That's funny."

You're not sure what's so funny about it, but as Becca walks away with her teammates, you hear her ask, "So, is your cookie *nutritious* and *delicious*?" The girls giggle.

 Turn to page 47.

As you gently round the bend in the path toward Shopping Square, you see Megan riding toward you on her bike, a brown-wrapped box in her basket. "Hey," she says, eyeing the boxes in your own basket. "Whatcha got there?"

You hesitate before answering. You wonder if Megan will be upset that you started your own delivery business, but you decide to tell the truth. "I'm delivering cupcakes for Sweet Treats bakery," you say.

Megan nods. "I heard you were doing deliveries," she says. "I'm not getting as much work from Bravo Boutique now that you're working for them." She smiles, but you can hear the edge in her voice. "Well, gotta go," she says as she pushes off with her bike. "Work to do."

As Megan pedals away, a seed of worry forms in your mind. Will she try to get work from Sweet Treats bakery now, too? Will you have competition?

 Turn to page 58.

The next day, you and your friends launch into a craft-making frenzy. By the end of the night, your room is a mess, but you have a pile of pretty hair accessories to sell. You agree to meet at the Market on Saturday to set up a table and give your craft sale a go.

When you get to the Market on Saturday, Neely is already there—with a huge sign that says "Star Style Crafts! Hair accessories for $1." She has decorated the border of the sign with sparkly stars. She's a great artist.

"Cute!" you say. "I love the name 'Star Style.' Good thinking!"

But Shelby shows up carrying a sign, too. Hers says "Hair Flair! Headbands, barrettes, and more. $2.50."

Logan is right behind her carrying a smaller sign. There's no name on the sign, but she lists different prices: "Headbands $3, Barrettes $2, Scrunchies $1."

Uh-oh. Not only did you not settle on a business name, you also didn't settle on a price for your crafts. You sort of thought you'd figure it out when you got here, but now your friends are bickering about which sign to use.

 Turn to page 64.

Becca already has the cookie in her hand. How can you say no?

"Um, sure," you say. "Could you pay me back tonight at dinner?"

"Definitely," says Becca. "Thanks!" And then she's gone, cookie in hand, back to a group of soccer players who are hanging out in the bleachers.

By the time three more of those players have come to your table asking if they can have cookies and "pay you at dinner," you're wondering if you made the wrong decision. But it doesn't seem fair to let only some girls—and not others—pay you later, so you hand over the treats.

You count your money at the end of the game. You made almost eight dollars. That's not bad, but you *should* have about ten dollars. You hope that Becca and the other soccer players pay you tonight so that you can make back the money you lost on those cookies.

 Turn to page 48.

At dinner that night, you're about to bite into a burrito when you hear someone ask, "Hey, is your burrito *nutritious* and *delicious*?"

It's Becca. She grins at you, her brown eyes flashing. She obviously thinks she's hilarious, but she's starting to get on your nerves.

When another soccer player walks by and comments on your "nutritious and delicious" nachos, you groan.

It seems as if you've dug a hole for yourself with your "healthy" advertising campaign. Maybe Shelby was right. From now on, you'll have to let your delicious—but not so nutritious—treats speak for themselves!

The End

That night at the Star Student Center, you fill your tray with nachos and slide into a seat across from Logan.

"How's the bake sale going?" she asks, taking a bite of burrito.

You shrug. "Pretty good," you say. "I made some money, but a few girls still owe me." You search the cafeteria line to see if any of those girls are here. Two of them are—Becca and another soccer player you don't know.

"Here comes Becca now," you say to Logan. Becca is walking toward you, holding her tray with one hand and waving with the other. You wipe your mouth with your napkin, ready to say hello. But as Becca gets closer, you see that she's not waving to you at all. She walks right by to join the table of girls *behind* you.

Your stomach sinks. That feeling is still there after dinner, when you realize that none of the girls paid you back—except for Riley.

 Turn to page 53.

"You're probably right," you say to Shelby as you reach across the table to take down the lemonade sign. You're kind of embarrassed about it now, so you try to explain. "I thought the soccer players would want something healthy, and I figured lemonade was better than soda."

"Well, you know," says Shelby thoughtfully, "most of the soccer players have their own water bottles, but they could probably use refills. Maybe you could offer ice-cold water?"

You hesitate. "Maybe," you say, but the truth is, water sounds kind of boring to you. Plus, you wouldn't make much money selling it, right? You wish there was a way you could give the drink your own special twist.

 Turn to page 54.

Before you know it, the customer is on her way again, and you didn't have to say a word.

"Wow," you say to Shelby, "you're really good with customers. Where'd you learn how to do that?"

Shelby shrugs. "I don't know," she says, blushing a little. "I figure that as long as you're nice to customers, they'll be nice to you."

You grin. That's such a Shelby thing to say. She's a total people person, which makes her a great friend. Now you see that those people skills make her a good business-person, too.

As you pack up the last of your crafts and take down your price list, you turn to thank Shelby.

If you ask Shelby to help you and your business, turn to page 57.

If you think you've already learned enough from Shelby, turn to page 67.

You wouldn't even *have* this job if not for Megan, so you want to make sure you're not hurting her business—or her feelings.

"I'm sorry," you say. "I didn't mean to take all the work. I'd like to figure out a way to share it."

Megan's brown eyes instantly soften. "Thanks," she says, breathing a sigh of relief. "I was hoping you'd say that. Maybe we could work out a schedule or something?"

After talking it through, you and Megan agree to split the work fifty-fifty. She delivers on Mondays, Wednesdays, and Fridays, and you deliver on Tuesdays, Thursdays, and Saturdays. You tell the manager of Dream Décor so that she knows which girl will make deliveries on which days.

There's still plenty of work, but now you have some days *off*, too, which gives you a break.

 Turn to page 62.

As you head head back to your room at Brightstar House, you're kicking yourself for not making the girls pay for their treats at the bake sale. After all, it cost *you* money to make them.

Now you're afraid to set up your table again at the soccer field. Will everyone there expect you to keep giving them things for free?

You sigh. You made some money today, and you're that much closer to getting your genie costume. But you also learned an expensive lesson: You need to collect the money first, *before* you give away the treats you worked so hard to make. That's only fair, and it's smart business, too.

The End

That night at dinner, while you're enjoying lemon-pepper chicken at the student center, an idea strikes—the perfect "twist" for your healthy drink.

Just before Wednesday's soccer game, you set up your table at the sports center. This time, you replace your pitcher of lemonade with a pitcher of cold water—with fresh lemon slices bobbing among the ice cubes. You bring more lemons in a cooler, plus ice so that you can keep the water cold.

Your water looks so cool and refreshing that Riley and the other soccer players visit your table at halftime *and* after the game. They come to get a drink, but many of them end up buying trail mix or cookies, too. You end the afternoon with an empty water pitcher and a full cash box. Your idea was a success!

 Turn to page 60.

Before you answer Becca, you take a deep breath and think it through. Cookies cost fifty cents—twice as much as lemonade. You don't know Becca as well as you know Riley, so you're not sure she'll pay you back the money. But it doesn't seem right to treat your customers differently. You think fast and come up with a solution.

"Actually," you say, "I'd rather you pay me first for the cookies. But if you want some lemonade now, like Riley's having, you can pay me later for that."

There's an awkward moment of silence, while Becca's hand hovers over the cookie, but she slowly pulls it back and reaches for a cup of lemonade instead. "Okay," she says. "Thanks."

You're proud of yourself for coming up with a smart solution. And as it turns out, Becca finds some money in her duffel bag and comes back for not just one cookie, but *two*. Pretty soon, your cash box is full of money—over ten dollars. Add to that what you made at the nature center, minus the cost of the ingredients, and you made almost twenty dollars in just one day. Wow!

Turn to page 60.

"I'm sorry, Megan," you say, hands in the air. "But I really need the work right now. I'm saving for something important."

Megan looks as if she's about to reply, but she doesn't. She just turns around and gets back on her bike.

You feel awful. "Megan, wait!" you call to her.

Megan stops her bike, bracing herself with her feet against the sidewalk, but she won't look back at you.

"I just need to make deliveries for another week," you say. "Then I'll have enough money, and you can have all the business back. Okay?"

Megan doesn't say a word. She hesitates for just a moment before pushing off with one foot and pedaling away.

You sigh and reach out to open the door to Dream Décor.

 Turn to page 61.

"Shelby," you ask, "do you want to help me out during sales? I could really use you. I'm not as smart as you are about this customer stuff."

Shelby smiles at you, her dark eyes dancing. "Oh, I'd love that!" she says. "But don't be so hard on yourself. You're plenty smart. Asking for help when you need it is the smartest thing you can do."

You shrug. There Shelby goes again, making someone else feel good. You made the right decision in "hiring" her. With your creativity and Shelby's people skills, your business is sure to be a success!

The End

When Sweet Treats bakery calls on Saturday to say that they have a big delivery for you, you rush right over. Boy, do they *ever* have a big delivery! The counter is stacked high with cupcake boxes.

As you walk toward the counter, you catch sight of someone else stepping up beside you: Megan. "What are *you* doing here?" you ask.

"Same as you," she says. "Making deliveries." You can't miss the competitive gleam in her eye, something you haven't seen since the two of you were on a diving team together.

All right, you think to yourself. *Game on.*

"We're trying to get these over to Pet-Palooza for an open house," Jessica explains to you and Megan. "We'll give you fifty cents for every box you deliver."

Megan reaches for a stack of boxes. You know that her bike has a bigger basket than your scooter has, which means she can probably take more boxes per trip. The only way you can make as much money as she does is to either stack the boxes high in your basket *or* make more trips.

 If you stack the boxes high, turn to page 63.

 If you try to make more trips, turn to page 69.

Riley offers to help you carry your table and leftover treats back to your room. On the way, she asks if you'd mind swinging by the Girl Gear shop so that she can pick up some new soccer socks.

"No problem," you say. When you get to Girl Gear, you lean your bake sale table against the wall, just inside the door. Then you browse the sales rack, where you spot a cute T-shirt for just five dollars. What a deal!

By the time you and Riley leave the shop, you've managed to spend eleven dollars on the T-shirt, a Frisbee, and a cute baseball cap—all on sale, of course.

You have less cash in your cash box now, but you're pretty sure that you can make up that money next weekend if you hold another bake sale. After all, you're in business now, and the money is flowing.

Turn to page 66.

$5.00

$3.50

$2.50

After another six long days' worth of deliveries, you finally have enough money for that costume. Whew! Your legs are sore from scootering, but you feel a rush of energy as you walk into Bravo Boutique to buy your genie costume.

It's not till you get home that you realize that the genie costume doesn't come with *shoes*. You imagine the shoes that would go perfectly with the costume: a pair of gold ballet flats. You think you might even have seen a pair at Twinkly Toes shoe store.

Unfortunately, you're out of money now. And, if you keep the promise you made to Megan (that you'd quit making deliveries as soon as you bought the costume), you're also out of a job.

Hmm . . . Maybe it would have been smarter to share the delivery work with Megan. You wouldn't have made money as quickly, but you could have kept working longer and earned money for other things. You stare at your genie costume, wishing you could grant yourself just one wish— a do-over with Megan.

The End

Partnering up with Megan helps you remember what a good friend she is. The two of you start hanging out after dinner and doing homework together. You're sitting at Starlight Library one night telling her about the genie costume that you're working hard to save up money to buy.

"Sounds cool," she says. "I can't wait to see it!"

You realize then that you've never asked Megan what *she* does with the money she earns from deliveries. When you do ask, Megan's face falls. She fiddles with her pencil for a moment before answering. "I'm trying to pay for my schoolbooks for this year," she finally says. "My mom lost her job, and money has been tight."

Books? It never occurred to you that one of your friends might have to pay for her own schoolbooks. You look down at your science book and then realize that the one Megan is using is a library copy. "Oh," you say, not sure how to respond. "I'm sorry."

Megan shrugs. "It's okay," she says. "This book for Earth Science is the last one I have to buy this year. Then I can finally use my own book instead of coming here to the library. Just twenty more dollars to save. I can't wait!" She smiles brightly and then turns back to her schoolwork.

 Turn to page 68.

You grab just as many boxes as Megan does, and then you hurry out the door behind her. Megan looks over her shoulder and quickens her pace.

You make it to your scooter just as Megan reaches her bike. She places the boxes easily in her basket, climbs onto her bike, and pushes off, heading down the stone path toward Pet-Palooza on the other side of campus.

You stack the boxes in your own basket and cross your fingers, hoping they don't topple. You want to get to Pet-Palooza and back quickly, but you can't go too fast, or you'll lose the cupcakes. You take a deep breath and step onto your scooter.

 Turn to page 70.

"We need different prices because the headbands cost more to make and the scrunchies cost less," Logan says.

"It doesn't matter what your prices are if you don't have a great business name and a pretty sign to draw customers to your table," argues Neely.

"If you two keep arguing, you won't have to worry about customers—you'll scare them all away," Shelby points out.

When your first customer comes, all four of you jump to attention. "Hi!" says Shelby. "Can I help you?"

Before the customer can answer, Neely jumps in and says, "Everything is just a dollar here at Star Style—"

"Actually," Logan interrupts her, "the headbands are three dollars."

Neely whirls around to look at Logan, and the customer takes a big step back from the table. "Um, just looking today," she mumbles before scurrying away. Even Shelby can't convince her to stay.

If you take charge and give each friend a job to do, turn to page 89.

If you let your friends work things out on their own, turn to page 91.

You hold another bake sale the following Saturday—this time at the Market. There are so many girls shopping in the tents at the Market that you predict you'll do good business, and you do. You make fifteen dollars by early afternoon!

When your trail mix runs out, you decide to shut down your bake-sale stand and do a little shopping of your own. You saw a girl go by with the cutest stuffed pig. Now which tent did she find that in?

You wander the tents until you find the pig, along with a pink bracelet and a matching ring. Now that you're making money, you realize just how many things are out there that you *have* to have!

When you count your money again, though, you realize that you've already blown twelve of your fifteen dollars. You look down at the pig and feel more guilt than delight. What were you *thinking*?

 If you try to get your money back, turn to page 72.

 If you keep the pig but promise yourself that you're done spending money, turn to page 86.

"Thanks for the tip," you say to Shelby. You know it'll come in handy.

Sure enough, the second day of your sale, you have a customer come back to your table, wanting to return a scrunchie.

"We have a no-refund policy," you say, remembering Shelby's words. "Would you like to trade it for something else?"

The girl shakes her head. "Nope," she says. "I just want my money back."

There's an awkward pause. Finally, you shrug and reach into your money box.

The next time a customer asks for a return, you say again, trying to sound firm, "We don't offer refunds."

The customer stares at you for a moment and then says in a huff, "Then I won't be buying anything from you anymore. And my friends won't, either." She turns on her heel and storms off.

Sheesh! Your heart is pounding in your ears. Keeping customers happy may come easily for Shelby, but it sure isn't easy for you.

You decide to shut down your table early. You need to rethink your business before the whole thing goes down the drain. First order of business? Finding a partner. You set off in search of Shelby, hoping that she'll say yes.

The End

During the next two weeks, you keep thinking about Megan and her schoolbooks. The other thing on your mind is whether your genie costume will sell out soon. By Friday, you finally have enough money to buy it. *Phew!*

You go to Bravo Boutique and flip through the rack of costumes. Some of them are on sale now—Shelby's angel costume and a princess costume that's the same purple satin as the genie one. Unfortunately, your genie costume isn't on sale, but it's every bit as beautiful as you remember.

As you walk toward the cash register, you think again of Megan and how excited she is to buy that science book—something your parents bought for you weeks ago. You wish there was a way you could help her reach her goal. You glance at the money in your hand.

 If you buy the genie costume, turn to page 71.

 If you use some of your money to help Megan, turn to page 74.

You decide that you're going to have to make more trips than Megan if you want to make just as much money. That means you're going to have to go *fast*.

You fill your basket with boxes and then hit the path. You veer through the crowd of girls in front of the student center, hollering "On your left!" and "Coming through!" You fly over the narrow wooden bridge, watching the boxes in your basket shake and shimmy with every bump.

You get to Pet-Palooza before Megan does, which is quite a feat. You grab the boxes out of your basket and practically toss them to Amber, a friend of yours who volunteers at the pet daycare center.

"Thanks!" Amber says, and then she adds something else—which you don't hear because you're already back on your scooter and rounding the corner of the building. "WAIT!" you finally hear her call again.

You groan. You don't have time for conversation, but Amber seems to have something really important to say. You turn around and wheel back toward her. She's standing there with one of the cupcake boxes open, holding it out for you to see. She doesn't look happy.

 Turn to page 112.

With every bump in the path, the tower of boxes in your basket jiggles. You're so busy watching the boxes that you don't see the squirrel darting across your path.

You swerve at the last minute, and out of the corner of your eye, you see a cupcake box start to s-l-i-d-e off the stack. You reach out your hand to grab it, throwing yourself off balance. You drop a foot and steady yourself, your heart pounding in your ears.

Slow down, you scold yourself as you try to catch your breath.

You can see Megan's bike ahead of you, disappearing around a bend in the path. Your heart sinks.

The next time you see Megan, you're just entering Five Points Plaza, and she's coming back from Pet-Palooza, her basket empty. As she zooms past you, she smiles in an "eat my dust" sort of way.

 If you speed up, turn to page 82.

 If you keep going slowly, turn to page 75.

You buy the costume, plus an inexpensive pair of gold flats to match, and hurry back to your room. Megan made you promise that you'd call her when you bought the costume so that she could come see it, so you do. When you hear her knock on the door, you open it—wearing your genie costume.

"Whoa!" Megan says, catching her breath. "I love it!"

You twirl around so that Megan can get the full effect while she laughs and claps her hands. "You saved enough money. Yay for you!" she says.

"Thanks!" you say, thinking again what a great friend Megan is. She's so happy about your purchase even though you know she's struggling to save money for things of her own. You wonder for a minute if you could have helped her more.

Maybe I still can, you tell yourself. You have your costume now, but you still have a job, too—thanks to Megan. You decide that starting next week, you'll offer some of the money you earn to Megan to help with the cost of her science book. She helped you, and now you hope you can help her, too.

The End

You go back to the tent where you bought the pig, hoping to get your money back. The girl behind the table shakes her head. "All sales are final," she says, pointing to a sign hanging above the stand.

You rub your eyes. How did you not see that sign before?

Your shoulders slump as you leave the table, the pig dangling from your hand. You bump right into your friend Isabel, who loves to shop and spends a lot of time at the Market.

"What's wrong?" she asks. "You look like you just lost your puppy."

"More like I just found my pig," you say with a half-hearted smile. "And I'm stuck with him now—no returns."

Isabel nods knowingly. "Buyer's regret?" she asks. "I know how that goes. I don't bring money to the Market anymore. That way, I'm not tempted to buy things I don't need. If I still want something by the time I walk back to my room for money, I *might* come back and get it."

That's smart, you think, wondering why you couldn't have run into Isabel before you bought the ridiculous pig.

 Turn to page 88.

You stop walking. Slowly, you turn around and head back toward the rack of costumes. You hang up the genie costume and take another look at the princess costume, which is half price now. As you stroke the fabric, an idea forms in your mind . . .

Half an hour later, you show up at the library—a little late. You search for Megan. There she is!

As you sit down across the table from her, you say, "Sorry. I had to run to Bravo Boutique to buy my costume."

Megan's jaw drops. "You did it?" she asks. "You saved enough for the genie costume?"

"Sort of," you say. You don't tell her that you bought the princess costume instead. You're pretty sure that with Neely's sewing skills, she can help you turn the princess dress into the billowy pants of a genie costume, but first things first. "As a new genie," you say, "I want to grant you a wish." You hand an envelope across the table to Megan.

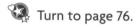 Turn to page 76.

Every muscle in your body wants to kick into gear and fly past Megan on your scooter. If you give in to that urge, though, you'll risk dropping the cupcakes. Instead, you decide to take it slow. That's the only smart choice.

When you reach Pet-Palooza, you carefully unload your cupcakes and walk them to the door.

"Wait, I'll help!" a familiar voice calls out. You look up and see your friend Amber walking toward you. You're not surprised to see her here. Amber loves animals and spends a lot of time volunteering at the pet daycare center.

"Thanks for delivering these safely," says Amber.

As she disappears through the doorway of Pet-Palooza, you climb back onto your scooter. You stop to think about the quickest path back to the student center. Now that you've delivered the cupcakes, you don't have to go slow. Should you cut through the grass or stick to the stone path?

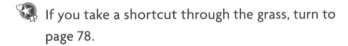 If you take a shortcut through the grass, turn to page 78.

 If you take the path back, turn to page 81.

Megan opens the envelope and pulls out a card you made. You drew a picture of a science book on the front, and inside, you tucked the twenty dollars that was left over after you bought the half-price costume. "For your science book," you say as Megan opens the card.

Megan is speechless for a moment. Then she shakes her head and tries to hand the money back. "Thanks so much," she says, "but I can't take this."

"It's a loan," you say, holding up your hand. "You can pay me back later. But now you can buy the book right away."

Megan stares at you, her brown eyes brimming with emotion, and then nods. "Thanks," she says, her voice thick. "That's really nice."

"No problem," you say. "We're partners, right?"

Megan nods again and gives you a grateful smile.

"Partners," she says.

As you flip open your own book, you feel a flutter of happiness inside, knowing you made the right choice—the smart choice—and helped a good friend.

The End

You figure you can save time if you cut across the grass behind U-Shine Hall.

You start scootering around the bushes, but it doesn't take you long to realize that your scooter is worthless in the grass. You hop off and lug your scooter the rest of the way.

When you reach the path, you set your scooter down and step back on, but your scooter won't budge. You look down and see that the wheels are full of grass. Now what?

If you leave your scooter here and run to the bakery on foot, turn to page 80.

If you call it quits, turn to page 85.

You just can't bring yourself to ask your friends for money. Instead, you sort through your closet, determined to make do with what you have.

You choose a pair of plain black flats. They don't really match your shiny gold-and-purple costume, but at least they don't clash. Hopefully no one will even notice them.

The night of the costume party, you walk with Shelby to Party Place. Shelby is wearing her angel wings and halo, which suit her perfectly. You meet Logan at the door, too, dressed as a cat from head to toe—er, paw.

And Neely? She's on the dance floor wearing a gold sequined top and flared gold pants, doing some disco moves. "She's a seventies dancer," explains Shelby with a giggle. "Doesn't she look great?"

Neely sees you and pulls you onto the dance floor, too. "I love your costume!" she says.

After a moment of dancing, Neely adds, "Hey, I know a way to make your costume even *better*."

 Turn to page 111.

You can't bring yourself to quit now, so you hide your scooter behind a bush and run to the bakery. You don't know how many deliveries you can make on foot, but you have to try.

You see Megan on her bike, riding toward you with another basketful of boxes. She gives you an odd look as she passes, probably wondering where your scooter is, but you don't have time to explain—and you're too out of breath.

You're wheezing by the time you reach the bakery, but you fill your arms with boxes and turn around to race back to Pet-Palooza. You move more slowly now, and by the time you're halfway there, your arms are aching. You have to stop twice to put the boxes down and rest.

Finally, you see Amber's friendly face in front of Pet-Palooza. "Where's your scooter?" she asks as she reaches out to take the boxes from you.

"Long story," you pant. "Tell you later."

 Turn to page 84.

The grass may be the shortest path, but it looks as if it would be a bumpy ride. Instead, you take the winding stone path back to the bakery, moving quickly now that your basket is empty.

When you get to the bakery counter, you take one fewer box of cupcakes—just to make the tower of boxes in your basket a little safer. Then you head to Pet-Palooza, going slowly and even taking a second to wave at Megan as she flies past you again on her bike.

You have time to make just two deliveries of cupcakes before the boxes are gone, but you feel okay about that. You made some smart choices—and some money. You don't have enough to buy your costume yet, but you're getting there. If there's one thing you've learned from the delivery business, it's that there *aren't* any shortcuts to success.

The End

The look on Megan's face makes you angry, and now you're determined to catch up with her.

You veer around a patio table, keeping your eye on the path ahead. You're moving so fast that when a girl gets up from her chair and steps in front of you, you don't have time to shout "Look out!" You make a sharp turn with your scooter—right toward the fountain.

You hit your hand brake and lurch forward. Then you see—in slow motion—the stack of cupcake boxes fly out of your basket and over the wall of the fountain. You hear the *splash* and feel the spray of water on your face as the boxes disappear into the frothy water.

There's a moment of total silence. Then girls start rushing toward you from all directions. "Are you okay?" they ask. "What happened? Why were you going so fast?"

You can't speak. You're considering diving into the fountain to rescue the cupcakes. When you see a soggy cake pop up to the water's surface, you know it's too late.

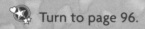 Turn to page 96.

You're exhausted, but you have to walk back to the bakery. You decide to stop for your scooter on the way. But when you reach the bushes where you left it, it's not there.

You search frantically under and around the bushes, scratching your arms in the process, but the scooter's gone. Did someone steal it?

That's it—you can't take it anymore. You sit back in the grass and burst into tears.

"Are you okay?" someone asks, resting a hand on your shoulder. It's Megan, her bike parked on the path beside you. She's the last person you want to see right now, but when she asks you what happened, you tell her—and she's amazingly nice about it.

"I'll help you find your scooter," she promises.

"But what about the bakery?" you ask, wiping your face and then pushing yourself up off the ground.

"I delivered the last of the cupcakes," Megan says. "So it's time to go get paid. How about if we walk together?"

 Turn to page 87.

"That's it," you say out loud. "I'm done." You want to fling your useless scooter into the bushes, but instead, you lug it down the path toward the plaza. You lean the scooter against a patio table and plunk yourself down in a chair.

You're still sitting there fifteen minutes later, staring at the bubbly fountain, when Megan coasts on her bike into the plaza. "I just delivered the last box of cupcakes," she proudly announces.

"Good for you," you snap.

Megan rolls her bike backward a few inches. "Sheesh," she says. "Are you really that bent out of shape about it?"

You sigh. "Sorry," you say. "It's just been a bad day."

But has it really? a voice in your head asks. You lost this silly competition with Megan, but you made a successful delivery of cupcakes, which means money to add to your savings. You already have about half of what you need for the genie costume, which is great. So it's time to stop beating yourself up and start counting the things you've done *right*.

You hold your hand out to Megan. "Truce?" you ask.

"Truce," she agrees. As you shake hands, you wonder if maybe it's time to stop competing against Megan and start working *with* her. You're both pretty good at this delivery thing. Maybe together, you could be even better.

The End

You're too embarrassed to return the pig. You'll just have to keep it—and try to spend less money from here on out. But that's easier said than done. You're super hungry by the time you leave the Market, so you stop at a hot dog stand and spend another dollar or two. Now you're almost broke—and completely depressed.

As you shuffle down the hall of Brightstar House toward your room, wondering why you even bothered to hold a bake sale today, you run into Logan. She quickly sees that something's wrong. "What is it?" she asks. "Didn't your sale go well?"

You shake your head. "That's the problem," you say. "The sale *did* go well, but I spent just about everything I made. I'm out of control!"

Logan giggles, but then she quickly covers her mouth. "Sorry," she says. "It's just that I know exactly how you feel. We *all* have trouble saving money sometimes. Do you want to see what helps me?"

You nod. Logan is usually good for some smart advice.

 Turn to page 92.

Megan pushes her bike beside you as you walk the path to the student center. When you get to the bakery, Jessica congratulates both of you on your quick deliveries. She counts out two stacks of dollar bills based on the number of boxes that each of you delivered.

Megan's stack of bills is bigger than yours, but it doesn't matter now. You're thinking about how much money you'll need to buy a new scooter, and the money you and Megan earned today combined won't even begin to pay for that.

As you leave the student center, Megan counts out some bills from her stack and hands them to you.

"What's that for?" you ask.

"We should split the profit down the middle," Megan says. "You did just as much work as I did. I just happened to have a bigger basket." She smiles, and then she promises again that you'll find your scooter. "We'll look for it together," she says.

Together. That sounds nice. You wish you'd been smart enough to ask Megan to work together in the first place. She's a great partner—and a great friend.

The End

You tell Isabel about your plan to make enough money for the genie costume. "But it seems like the more money I *make*, the more I spend!" you groan.

Isabel holds up her index finger, letting you know that she has an idea. She tucks a red curl behind her ear and reaches down to pull something out of her purse—a picture torn out of a sales flyer. It's of a zebra-print bedspread with red pillows thrown on top.

Isabel gently smooths out the creases in the ad. "This is part of my dream bedroom," she says. "I've been saving for the bedspread for a month. I carry a picture of it so that any time I want to buy something else, I remember what I *really* want. It helps me save money."

"It looks cool!" you say, easily picturing the bedspread in Isabel's room, which is full of bold prints and patterns. "I wonder if that would work for me," you add, thinking out loud.

Isabel looks up. "You mean a picture of your genie costume?" she asks. "I bet it would. I'd even take the picture for you." She reaches into her purse again and pulls out a camera.

"Right now?" you ask.

"Why not?" she says with a bright smile.

 Turn to page 90.

You don't want to tell your friends what to do, but as the girl who started this business, you know you have to do *something*.

"This isn't working," you say to your friends. "Maybe if we each have a different job to do, things will go better."

You look at your friends, thinking about their different strengths. Neely is super creative, Logan is smart about math and other subjects, and Shelby is great with people. If each one of them focuses on her strengths, you'll have a pretty good team.

"Neely," you say, "I love your creative sign and the name you gave our business. And, Logan, I think you're right about prices—we should charge more for the crafts that cost more to make. And Shelby? You're so good with customers. I think you should be the one to greet them."

You hold your breath, waiting for your friends to disagree, but they don't. Each one of them looks proud, actually, and happy with her new role.

Neely gets to work making a new sign with the name of the business and the price that Logan gave each craft. Shelby greets customers while Logan handles the money. And you? You sit back, feeling pretty smart about—and proud of—the way you just handled things.

 Turn to page 95.

You walk with Isabel to Bravo Boutique, lugging your leftover treats. Isabel takes a few pictures of the genie costume, and when she e-mails them to you later, you grin from ear to ear. The costume looks great!

You print out the photos and put them up around your room. You put one in your purse, and you put another one in your bake-sale cash box as a reminder that any money you earn should stay in the box—or at least in your piggy bank.

Speaking of pigs, the stuffed pig helps you with your savings plan, too. You prop it up on your desk as a reminder of what *not* to buy.

 Turn to page 93.

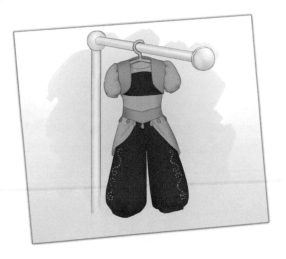

The next couple of business transactions don't go very well, either. When a customer asks how much the headbands cost, neither Neely nor Logan says a word. They stare at you, and the customer does, too.

"Um . . . two dollars?" you say. It sounds like more of a question than an answer.

The customer shrugs and hands over a couple of dollars, but you don't feel very good about the sale. You're pretty sure Neely thinks you're charging too much and Logan thinks you're not charging enough. The afternoon drags on, with the tension among your friends hanging like a storm cloud above your table.

You sell more hair accessories that afternoon, but you decide not to do another sale tomorrow. One craft sale among your bickering friends is enough. Maybe business and friendship just don't mix.

To cheer up your friends, you decide to give them each a gift: a cutely wrapped box of hair accessories with a note that says, "To friends with star style. Thanks for sticking with me at the sale!"

When you're done wrapping the boxes, you turn to your next creative project—looking for something you can wear to the costume party. You're not going to earn enough money to buy that genie costume, so you're going to have to get creative with the clothes in your own closet.

The End

You follow Logan to her room, and she shows you two glass jars sitting on a shelf in her closet. One is labeled "spend" and the other is labeled "save." The "save" jar has a lot more money in it than the "spend" jar.

"Every time I get money," Logan explains, "I put half of the money in each jar. That way I always have money to spend, but I'm saving, too."

Logan's savings plan seems so simple, but it's pretty smart, too. "You might want a third jar," she adds. "You'll need supply money—you know, for buying ingredients and things."

"Uh-huh," you say, wishing you had a notebook where you could write all this down.

"Just remember 'S, S, S'—'save,' 'spend,' and 'supplies,'" says Logan, as if reading your mind.

"Got it," you say. You're excited to get started!

 Turn to page 94.

You spend the few dollars you have left on trail mix ingredients, and the next day, you hold another sale. You go back to the Market, which is risky, because you're tempted to buy things there. But whenever you see something you want, you look at the photo of your costume—and you stand strong.

By the end of the *next* weekend, you've officially saved enough money for the genie costume—plus a pair of matching gold ballet flats. You march proudly toward Bravo Boutique.

Your purse will be back to empty soon, but you know how to fill it again—and how to save what you earn for something you really want. You've learned a lot about money, thanks to Logan, Isabel, and one stuffed pig.

The End

You stop at Neely's room next. You think she saves empty jars for storing things like art supplies. Sure enough, she pulls a few from a box in her closet.

You make colorful sticker labels for the jars, and you set them on your closet shelf. Now all you have to do is make some money to put *in* them.

You empty out your piggy bank to buy more treat and trail mix ingredients, and you hold bake sales for the next two weekends. After each sale, you have fun dividing the money among the three jars. And when you need to make treats for the next sale, you know just where to find the money for ingredients. You pour some out of your "supplies" jar and go shopping.

After two weeks, you have enough money for that genie costume. Part of you is kicking yourself for not having raised the money sooner (the stuffed pig trots across your mind), but the other part of you is proud for having the money now. You run to Bravo Boutique and head to the costume rack. You flip through a few costumes, searching for yours, but . . . it's *gone*!

 Turn to page 97.

On Sunday, when you and your friends set up your craft table again at the Market, Neely brings the new sign she made—plus a stack of flyers. "I thought I could do more advertising," she says. "If I hand these out to people, maybe I can get more of them to visit our table."

"Great idea!" you say. "Thanks, Neely."

As she steps away from the table, Shelby leans in toward you and says, "Hey, can I talk to you about something?"

"Sure. What's up?" you ask.

"Well . . ." Shelby begins, hesitating. "Kayla and her friends Tiara and Ruby heard about our new business, and she wonders if they can join us. Do you think we need more help?"

You don't know Tiara and Ruby, but you really like Kayla. Do you think you should make your business bigger by adding more people?

If you say yes, go online to innerstarU.com/secret and enter this code: PAYS2BSMART

If you say no, turn to page 98.

The scooter ride back to the bakery—with an empty basket—is the longest of your life. Just before you reach the student center, Megan races past you again with another basketful of cupcakes. You don't even look at her. You're too mad at her for ruining your cupcake-delivery career.

Then you catch yourself. Megan didn't ruin your career—*you* did. You knew you were going too fast, but you did it anyway. There were plenty of cupcakes for you both to deliver, but you had to compete with Megan and try to match her box for box.

By the time you get to the bakery, your head is hanging low. Logan is arranging a tray of cookies behind the counter. "What happened?" she asks, her eyes filled with concern.

You tell her the whole story—it just comes pouring out. "To make a long story short," you say afterward, "I made some really dumb decisions."

 Turn to page 99.

When you see that your costume is gone, you nearly burst into tears. This is so unfair!

The cashier working behind the checkout counter sees the expression on your face. "What were you looking for?" she asks, stepping around the counter to help you.

You describe the genie costume, and the cashier nods. "We just sold our last one this morning," she says apologetically. "But we might be able to find you something like it online. Or do you want to look at the costumes on our sales rack? There's still some really cute stuff."

If you decide to shop online, turn to page 100.

If you check out the sales rack, turn to page 102.

"I don't know, Shelby," you say. "I think we're doing okay, just the four of us, don't you? Plus, I don't know Tiara and Ruby."

Shelby breathes a sigh of relief. "That's what I thought, too," she says, "but I had to ask. I promised Kayla I would."

It makes you feel better knowing that Shelby backs your decision. You trust her opinion. And your business is doing great just the way it is. Neely's flyers bring in even more customers, and pretty soon your cash box is full.

You count out the money at the end of the day and split it among the four of you, leaving some of the money in the box to buy more supplies.

 Turn to page 101.

"We all do dumb things sometimes," Logan says. "But you're doing one really smart thing."

"What's that?" you ask, raising your eyes to meet hers.

"Admitting your mistakes," she says. "If you admit your mistakes, you can learn from them, and you probably won't make the same ones again." Logan grins, and you muster up a small smile, too.

"Come on," she says, waving you behind the counter. "Let's tell Jessica what happened and get it over with. And then I'll buy you a cupcake."

You snort. "No, thanks," you say, laughing. "I don't think I'll need to see a cupcake again for a *very* long time."

The End

The cashier pulls up the store's website and searches for "genie costume." The picture of your purple costume pops up with the words "sold out" splashed across it, which just about breaks your heart. But then you see a costume that's a lot like yours, except it's turquoise and has a hat with a veil.

"Ooh," you say, "I like it!"

"It's beautiful," the clerk says, "but it's five dollars more. Is that okay?"

You sigh. You emptied out your jar before coming here, which means you'll need to make more money before you can order this costume. But five dollars isn't very much. You think you can earn it pretty quickly.

 Turn to page 105.

You and your friends meet one night during the week to make more hair accessories, and you hold two sales the following weekend. When you count out the profits at the end of the weekend, you realize you have almost enough money to buy that genie costume.

Shelby's excited, too, because she has decided to buy the angel costume at Bravo Boutique.

"I hope it's still there!" she says, a shadow of worry darkening her eyes.

You're a little worried about that, too. You haven't checked on your genie costume all week. Has someone snatched it up?

You glance back into the cash box. There's a wad of bills in there set aside to buy more supplies. If you split that money between you and Shelby, you can both buy your costumes—today.

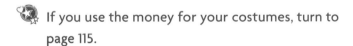 If you use the money for your costumes, turn to page 115.

 If you save it for supplies, turn to page 104.

You're ninety-nine percent sure there's nothing for you on the sales rack, but it can't hurt to look, can it?

You flip through some costumes that you recognize: an angel, a princess, and a superhero. Then you come to one you *haven't* seen before. It's a magician's costume, complete with a shiny cape and a hat with a rabbit in it. You pull out the rabbit, which is much cuter than that stuffed pig sitting on your desk at home.

You check the price tag of the costume. It's half off!

Do you like this costume more than the genie costume? No, but you like it just as much. And if you buy it, you'll be performing a little bit of money "magic." You'll go home with a costume you like, plus a little extra money, too. Maybe you can put it back in your "save" jar for something else. How smart is that?

Pretty smart, you say to yourself as you head toward the cash register. *Pretty smart.*

The End

You're tempted to spend the supply money on costumes, but you've made smart business decisions so far—and you don't want to blow it now. You'll need more supplies if you want your business to keep growing, and you'll have plenty of money for costumes after one more sale.

"Should we go check on our costumes?" you ask Shelby. "Just to be sure they're still there?"

Shelby must think that's a good idea, because she's already running out the door ahead of you. And when you get to Bravo Boutique and see both costumes still hanging on the rack, Shelby breathes the loudest sigh of relief.

"I wish we could make the money we need before next weekend," she says.

"Well," you say thoughtfully, "maybe we can. Who says we have to wait till next weekend to hold a craft sale?"

You visit Logan and Neely to see if they'd be willing to hold a craft sale midweek, and when they agree, you put the plan into motion.

 Turn to page 119.

You're hurrying out the door of the shop just as Shelby is coming in. "Hey!" she says, holding the door for you. "Did you get your costume?"

"No," you say. "It's sold out."

Shelby's jaw drops. "Oh, no!" she says. "I'm sorry."

"I'm not," you say. "I found something better online, but I have to make a little more money before I can buy it. I'm off to get more bake sale ingredients."

Shelby smiles. "That's great!" she says. "It reminds me of something my aunt always says: When life hands you lemons, make lemonade."

You giggle. "Nutritious and delicious," you joke. "Thanks, Shelby." And then you're off. You have business to do and a costume to buy. This time, you're not going to waste any time. That costume is *yours*.

The End

A half hour later, Shelby is trying on her costume in your room while you cut the price tag off your own. That's when you realize that your costume doesn't come with *shoes*.

"Does yours come with slippers or flats or anything?" you ask Shelby.

"Nope," she says. "But it goes all the way to the floor. I can wear any shoes I want. No one will see them!"

When Shelby turns around and sees your costume laid out on the floor, she realizes your dilemma. "Oh," she says. "You could use some gold slippers with yours."

Shelby scans the shelf of shoes in your closet.

"I don't think I have anything like that," you say, digging through a pile of shoes in the corner.

"They have some cute ballet flats at Twinkly Toes," Shelby suggests.

"Yeah, but . . ." You reach for the piggy bank on your dresser and shake it upside down. Nothing falls out. Now what?

 Turn to page 110.

The day of the costume party, you parade down the hall of Brightstar House with a black cat and an angel by your side. You, Logan, and Shelby knock on Neely's door to see if she's ready.

Neely opens the door with a curly wig on her head full of Star Style hair accessories. She's wearing a hairstylist's apron, too, stocked with brushes, combs, and spray bottles. You burst out laughing.

"You haven't seen the best of it," says Neely with a smile. When she turns around, you see an advertisement stuck to her back. It says "Star Style" in big fancy letters, and "Visit us at the Market!" underneath.

"Our business is doing so well," Neely says, "that I thought I'd use my costume to spread the word!"

"You're so smart," you say to Neely, adjusting a barrette in her hair. "And so stylish."

Neely links arms with you and the others. "We're smart and stylish," she says. "We're Star Style!" Then you head off to the party, advertising your business all the way.

The End

"We'll just have to make more hair accessories to sell," says Shelby with a good-natured shrug.

"With what supplies?" you ask, your heart sinking like a deflated balloon.

"Oh, yeah," says Shelby, frowning. "Maybe Neely and Logan wouldn't mind buying the batch of supplies this time."

Even as she mentions the idea, you can tell that Shelby doesn't think it's a great one. Asking friends for money is so, well, *awkward*. But Neely and Logan aren't just friends. They're business partners, too, right?

 If you ask your friends for help, turn to page 114.

If you make do with what you have, turn to page 79.

Neely steps off the dance floor and hikes up one of her pant legs to show you what she's wearing on her feet: gold satin flats. She kicks them off and offers them to you. "They'll look great with that costume," she says. "And I can wear yours—no one will see them under these long pants!"

When Neely convinces you to make the trade, you confess to her that you've been wanting a pair of gold flats but didn't have the money.

"You should have asked!" says Neely. "I could have loaned you some money—or loaned you these shoes. I've had them for months."

Now you wonder why you *didn't* ask. "You're a great friend," you say to Neely, "and you, Shelby, and Logan make great business partners, too."

"Partners?" Neely asks, cupping her hand to her ear to hear the beginning of the next song. "I thought you'd never ask." She grabs your hand and leads you back out onto the dance floor.

The End

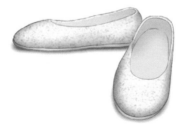

You look into the box of cupcakes. One of them is pretty cute: it's decorated like the face of a white puppy. The other three are less cute. The frosting faces on them are smeared and smushed, and you see globs of frosting on the lid of the box and around the sides.

"Did you drop these or something?" Amber asks.

You stare at the ground. "Not exactly," you say, which is true. But you know the cupcakes are ruined because of your crazy scooter ride. And you know you have to replace them.

"I'll take them back," you say, reaching for the box. "And I'll bring you new ones."

Amber doesn't argue. She hands you the other boxes, too, all of which contain cupcakes with smeared faces.

You take the ride back to the bakery slowly, trying to fix your own face. You feel like crying, but you're not going to. You're going to march into the bakery, be honest about what happened, and offer to pay for the cupcakes by delivering new ones—as many new ones as it takes—for free.

You made a mistake today, but you're smarter because of it, and you're determined to do a better job *next* time.

The End

You call Neely and Logan and ask if they can both stop by your room. You're nervous, but you think you've figured out a way to make this money thing work.

When both Logan and Neely are sitting in front of you, you take a deep breath and dive in. "Here's the thing," you say. "I'm wondering if you could loan me some money—to buy more supplies for the business."

Logan is confused at first. "But we just got paid!" she says. "Don't you have any left?"

You explain the costume and shoe situation, and then you assure your friends that if they loan you the money, you'll pay them back with a little extra—*interest,* you think it's called.

"No problem," says Neely. "I'm loaded." She shakes her purse, which sounds as if it's full of coins. "Listen to all that gold," she says with a grin.

"What are you, a pirate?" jokes Logan. Then she turns back to you. "Count me in, too," she says. "After all, what are friends for?"

You jump up and hug your friends, and soon you're all on your way to Sparkle Studios to buy supplies for your next craft sale.

 Turn to page 116.

"You know, Shelby," you say, reaching for the cash, "the whole point of starting a business was to raise money for those costumes. We have enough money now, if we use our supply money, too. What do you think?"

Shelby looks doubtful. "I don't know," she says. "What about Logan and Neely?"

"We can pay them back later," you say. "We'll take a week or two off from crafting, and when it's time to buy more supplies, you and I can chip in more than the others."

Shelby glances at you, then at the cash, and then back at you. When you see the twinkle in her eye, you know she's on board with your plan. You grab the cash—and Shelby's hand—and head off to Bravo Boutique.

 Turn to page 106.

After holding craft sales the following weekend, you finally earn the money you need for the shoes.

The night of the costume party, you walk through the doors of Party Place in a shimmery purple genie costume and matching gold flats. You remember how much work went into getting the costume, and with every step you take, you feel a surge of happiness—and pride.

You search the crowded room for your friends.

There they are! Logan is sipping punch by the snack table, her long black cat tail waving back and forth. She's talking with Shelby, who lights up the room in her angel costume.

And Neely? She's already on the dance floor, dressed like a pirate. She must have pulled the outfit together at the last minute from things she had in her own closet. She's so creative!

 Turn to page 118.

You hit the dance floor with Neely and show off some magic genie moves. Shelby floats across the floor like an angel, and Logan prances around like a cool cat. When the four of you finally take a break to sit and sip fruit punch, you thank Logan and Neely again for loaning you money for supplies.

"You were true friends," you say to them. "Thank you for helping me out."

"No, thank *you*," says Neely. "You gave me a great idea for a costume! And with the interest you paid on the loan, I scoped out some more sunken treasure." She opens up a pouch dangling from her belt and tosses each of you a gold coin—chocolate, of course.

You giggle as you unwrap the foil-covered candy. You pop it into your mouth, savoring the sweet taste of chocolate and of success—the success of a business that wouldn't have made it this far without the smarts and support of your friends.

The End

You buy supplies on Monday afternoon and get together with your friends that night to make more hair accessories. Logan suggests that you hold your sale at the Good Sports Center on Wednesday, during a soccer game.

When you get to the sports center, you see girls selling snacks and drinks, but no crafts. At first, you worry that no one will buy from your table. Who needs hair accessories at a soccer match?

As it turns out, plenty of girls do—the soccer players themselves! You sell more scrunchies at the soccer field than you ever have before. Most of the players wear their hair in ponytails while they play, and the green scrunchies you made match the Innerstar U uniforms. Perfect!

By the end of the night, you've finally made enough money to buy that costume, plus cute shoes to match.

 Turn to page 108.